GW01057475

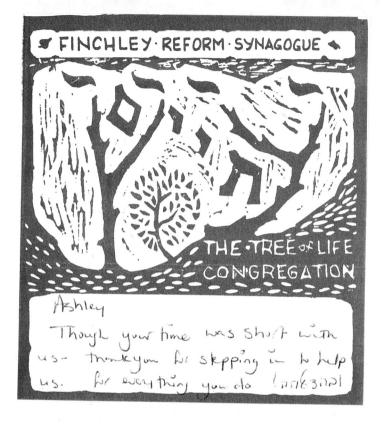

FINCHLEY · REFORM · SYNAGOGUE

עץ חיים

THE · TREE ᴏꜰ LIFE
CON·GREGATION

Ashley

Though your time was short with
us - thankyou for skipping in to help
us. for everything you do בהצלחה

THE STOVE

Short Stories

Jakov Lind

sh

THE MENARD PRESS
(ANTHONY RUDOLF)
8 THE OAKS
WOODSIDE AVENUE
LONDON N12 8AR
tel: 0181-446-5571

Published by The Sheep Meadow Press
distributed by
Persea Books
225 Lafayette St.
New York, N.Y. 10012

Printed in the United States of America

Library of Congress Cataloging in Publication Data

Lind, Jakov, 1927—
    The stove.

    Contents: 1. The cheat— 2. The lie— 3. The theft—[etc.]
    I. Title.
PR6062.I45S8   1983   823'.914   82-10824
ISBN 0-935296-26-3
ISBN 0-935296-27-1 (pbk.)

To Mary Kaplan

CONTENTS

THE STOVE

DEAR BUCI,

The other day I conceived a brilliant new idea and I am writing you immediately to tell you about it.

Let's go into stoves. Dutch stoves. I have found three good reasons why we must, can and should go into stoves.

First proposition: The Kingdom of God on this earth lies not in the heavens nor in the waters beneath them, but somewhere in the middle, between heaven and the deep. Whatever this earth yields, therefore, we must love and worship, and what is rarest in this world is what attracts us most. Hence we love jewels—rare stones, diamonds—gold, silver, exquisite houses, beautiful gardens, in short, the good life with all its luxuries. Riches are hoarded by the middle class, who need our stoves.

Second proposition: It is evident and therefore true that all things created, men included, have a temporal nature. Because of time we invented calendars and clocks. We must hurry. Since it is true that all that has been created owes its life to a Creator, we walk before Him in fear and humility. It follows we must not kill, give and take, buy and sell.

Third proposition: Without killing and without anyone on our side getting killed this time, we should get into stoves and not wait until everyone catches on to the idea. It will be too late. Life gets more expensive every day. Selling stoves, if and when they work, is an honest business that keeps people happy and warm. The Dutch stoves I want to buy in Amsterdam are the best of their kind ever made, a hundred percent profit is certain, and there may be more. The risks are nil. Let me know whether I can count on you. I need you, dear Buci. Yours,

A few days later I received the following:

Dear Cousin,
  It's not as easy as you would like it to be. My mind is open to all sorts of propositions, but let me start by criticizing you first: Who says the Lord's Kingdom lies in the middle and doesn't hang sideways upside–down? And why do you worship this earth, which is pure matter, and all it yields? Speak only for yourself. I, for my part, see a better quality of matter as the air gets thinner, higher up, the best still awaits us, and ultimately there is nothing better than the Infinite, the seat of the Holy One Himself. The earth might not last longer than a loaf of bread with a hungry man. What should a man do with luxuries? I like them in other men's homes. I prefer to enjoy them for a weekend than spend all year round with them. After a short time luxuries are no longer exciting; they become expensive to keep up and require too much attention. As for your insistence that we must hurry, I can't see the reason for this either. If we have no time, we are too late anyway; if we have a little time, we still have a little time longer to plan this business properly; and if we have a long time, which is my feeling, why hurry? To your last point: If we want to have real success we must be ready to sacrifice everything, even blood, but if we don't care for real success why go into business? Let me know what you think. If you go it alone and become rich, remember the various charities of which I am President. Remember also there is no hurry. If everyone wants to get into stoves, let them. The more stoves,

the more business, the more business, the more stoves. As long as there will be cold seasons we cannot lose.

Yours,

So I answered him:

Dear Buci,

You are a cousin of mine, and yet a fool. Last time I saw you you told me the grandfather we share beat you with his belt, because you ran away from school and home to your mother when you were four. Did he beat you over the head? How can you be so blockheaded, so rigid, so without sense? On the other hand, because of this one single beating, you might also have come to your senses faster than you would have otherwise and begun to see the light gradually. When I said let's hurry with the stoves, all I meant was let's not waste too much time. If I suggested God's Kingdom is in the middle, it is because everything that lies in the middle is good. Not too strong and not too weak, not too cold and not too hot, not too good and not too bad, and so on. Every sensible person will agree with me that extremes are harmful to body and soul in the long run. To sell stoves to the rich at the top we would need too much capital investment; to sell to the poor (who have no money) at the bottom would try our patience, mercy and love for our fellow-men. But if we sell them to those in the middle-income group, we shall be selling something they need above everything else. The masses need warmth in the winter and can afford it. My chances and yours to enter business, now that everyone becomes everyone else's trading partner, are greater than ever before. This is a time for trade and not for war. No one will be killed with our stoves; they don't blow up if you handle them properly. I don't know if you follow what's going on in this world? I do.

Yours,

And he writes back saying:

Dear Cousin,
    Still talking about stoves? Have you lost *your* mind? Don't
you know that everyone is selling stoves cheaper than we can,
because everyone shares his risk with investors while we are
only the two of us. We would need, relatively speaking, more
capital than Shell. We can't do it. We lack contacts, we have no
friends, no credit, no knowledge, no experience and, of course,
no stoves. We can't sell what we haven't bought yet. You can sell
even hot air, I agree, but you have to own it. You are a dreamer—
I have no time for your nonsense. Besides, it is absurd to think
people will buy your stoves, just because you believe it is good
for them to keep warm. Have you ever heard of someone doing
anything that is really good for himself? Sometimes it appears
that way, I agree; we think we act out of self-interest, but look
at it more closely, give it a closer view. Look at it as you would
look at your stoves. Examine the matter throughly. Look at all
the details and hidden pitfalls, note the unexpected technical
faults you might encounter and try to see deeper into the human
soul, into an interior that burns itself up without a drop of fuel,
only with remorse for the passing of time, and you will see that
no man acts for himself because it is good for him and rarely
good for others. But a man learns this only after he has acted.
Man is neither satisfied with or without warmth; he always
will need something he cannot obtain, will always be hungry
as the Behemoth, and will need more space than the Leviathan
itself. People will laugh at your stoves and you will waste more
of your time, which you can ill afford, as *you are* in a hurry to
judge by your letters.
                                                    Yours,

    So I didn't wait but wrote:

Dear Buci,
    If England can sell perfume in France, and Israel flowers in
Holland, and America wheat in the Ukraine, why can I not sell
stoves in this country? The "thermal situation," so to speak, in

this country is unbelievable and indescribable. All year round people somewhere are cold. Come winter they are very cold, yet they believe God wills that they should freeze. This is the tradition. Slowly, however, things are changing even in Europe. The change has come gradually. In World War II they lost their position in the colonies and their influence in the Commonwealth; they came back to these shores, retreating. Last time, at Suez, they tried to go back to the East (where it's warmer) and were prevented by their old ally, the United States. And as they lost their power in the world, they opened their gates to new ideas from the superally, America. First came Elvis Presley, who spawned the Beatles, who created a demand for drugs. Now our time has come. We must warm them in their homes. When they are comfortable we can also discuss other matters. How can a man open his eyes to God's glory when everything around him is frozen? But people who are warm at home sing Him a small Psalm, compose a poem in His honor, prepare to do good deeds. Dear Cousin, do you really think I am interested in business as such? All I want is to have everyone devote his time to study and singing, but because of inadequate central heating, useless and dangerous gaspipes and electric dreckfires in this country, His glow cannot enter the soul.

Yours,

His answer was silence. I had to write him again:

Dear Buci,

You haven't answered my letter, and we are at the end of January—the winter is nearly over. Soon the sun will shine us out of business. Decide—don't hesitate. Think simply and act quickly. There is a time for everything, provided we don't procrastinate. I made a practical proposition and you try to back out. Watch your step. The creditors are waiting and will eat us both alive and then you will be sorry. Wherever I go, I see creditors, people who look at me as if I owe them something. I haven't

paid my debt to society maybe. Hence the new idea. I have to
act, what good is it to think? What is His wisdom and His
mercy good for if not to search out the reason behind all reason
and the secret meaning behind all obvious meaning? I want to
supply people with life. Life is warmth. A stove is life—life
itself. To start with, my own life depends on it, and so should
everyone's. Am I different, less or more human than others? If
I wish to be warm and comfortable, I must also make it possible
for others. The money is unimportant, the main thing is to act
before the season is over. Don't let me wait longer than abso-
lutely necessary; I might change my mind and we would then
both regret it one day. Consider the stakes: no investment, no
outlay, no overheads, no transport versus accumulation of dead
capital, senseless war budgets, an expensive civil service, millions
killed on the roads. Our stove would have to compete with other
makes before it could lose, but we have no competition, all we
need do is act. Do you know the parable of the fox and the duck?
The fox wanted to catch the duck but the duck turned into a
wolf before the fox made his move, and after that, it was too
late—the fox had to run for his life.

Yours,

Soon afterwards came the following reply.

Dear Cousin,
    There are several possibilities we have not yet explored:
We must order the stoves without any guarantee that we can
sell them, find salesmen to sell stoves on which they have no
delivery date, ask the customer to pay in advance for a stove he
has neither seen nor heard of and maintains he doesn't even
need. These problems we have not yet given thought to. We
might be lucky and hit on a good way to guarantee something
without warranty, promise something without certainty, and so
on. I have given it long thought. We definitely cannot do it.
People don't know what they want, and everyone offers the same
goods at differing prices. How can you prove our stoves are

better? Can you prove it? You have to prove it not to me—I am
your cousin—but to the masses who are not of our family, and
the masses don't care to buy comforts just so *you* might feel
comfortable, and the masses don't suffer what hurts you pri-
vately. Consumers, dear Cousin, have few esoteric ideas; they
don't trust anything new, nor do you and I. If someone wants
to sell us a stove and it is new, we will refuse to buy it until we
have no choice. How can we make sure they will have no choice?
And who can tell whether they will want it afterwards? Let the
banks sell stoves to the people. They could finance them first,
so the masses could buy their stoves. Let me remind you it is
not our business to sell stoves either. The business is off.
No stoves.

> Yours,

I was furious and quickly replied to him:

Dear Buci,

I waited for weeks for your letter, or so it seems, and you
surprise me. You are a cynic. You are not one of us. We have the
same grandfather, we have the same blood, we are practically
brothers only once removed, we should at least be able to speak
the same language. My proposition is serious. My business may
be words (I have written many of them), and you have repaired
more faces with plastic than there is plastic to go around (I read
in the papers that you cut a bit of skin from your own calf when
you had to cover a harelip). We are both in the repair business,
as it were, but I would like to do something new and exciting.
All the noses you have straightened, all the chins you have
replaced do not change the total face; all the words I have had
printed haven't changed anyone's mind. We must not go on
forever neglecting our obvious duty to ourselves, to society, to
our children. Let's start now, not later. The stoves are cheap, of
excellent make, easy to install, economical to run and within ten
minutes can change anyone's atmosphere from freezing to
bearable. Who else can offer a system like ours? It has no faults.

A perfect mechanism. If there is a better system on the market,
let's buy it by all means, but in the meantime, until we find a
better one, let's sell ours. You are my future partner. We will
have a huge office in the West End. Sauna during lunchtime,
beautiful women serving cold tea, food prepared by Oriental
masters, playing chess all day long and only occasionally talking
on the telephone. I can hardly wait for your reply.

Yours,

And then I finally get the following:

Dear Cousin,
    I hesitated even with this answer, as writing to deaf ears
is like living in a tunnel with both exits blocked. You don't
understand what I am trying to do. I hesitate just because I want
to help, not harm, our interest. The longer we wait the easier
things will get. Time is on our side; we have more of it than we
need. Let's first invest in education and hygiene, a healthy body
makes for a healthy mind. In later generations people will be
more appreciative of our foresight. Now they don't need
warmth, for they first need to learn why they should want to be
warm. The human species has evolved slowly and the pace does
not change. Only people like yourself believe every day to be the
last, regard life as a temporal affliction and see the dust and ashes
and not the reincarnation of all flesh. There is no need to be
hasty in anything, all has its time and place. I am not ready for
it, nor are you.
    Why be rich if one can be poor? Why own a palace if all
one needs is a hut and less than that? Did Jonah not survive
inside a fish? You want to bring warmth into homes so people
can read your pious homilies, yet the first lesson has passed by
you: You need customers who believe in your stoves before you
can find customers. First create a demand, then you can supply it,
but if no one wants what you have, and those who want it can't
pay for it, what business are you in? I will become your partner
providing you don't sell the stoves, but give them away for

nothing, yet in such a business you won't need me—anyone can give away another man's property. Why aren't you more practical?

Yours,

So I wrote:

Dear Buci,
  I fail to understand your objections. Time is definitely on our side as you pointed out, provided we act fast. Our difference of opinion concerns only one important issue: when to act—now or later. Although time is on our side, we are not getting younger either, and time grows older with us by the hour. God might sell stoves better and cheaper than ours long after we are gone, but we are neither God nor a big corporation and must act soon. As you pointed out before, there are just the two of us. We are of the same family, share the same interests, yet again we are basically opposed. Your name is Buci and they call me Henry; we have the same ancestor in common, the same grandfather. Like Israel and Judah we cannot agree to whom Jerusalem will belong—to the man who conquers it with the sword or to him who longs to live in it only inside his mind. To own a town of peace—Jerusalem—cannot be an esoteric wish-dream, one has to live there, body and soul, or one will live somewhere else. When Israel was besieged, Judah had to come to his rescue. You will need me to bail you out of prison when the creditors get you, and I need your help now to stay out of prison. God knows how you can go on repairing people's faces forever. What difference does it make? A shorter nose doesn't always help. And I don't believe you make money, not with this kind of work. Let's work together instead. Start contacting the first customer, a man in the street. We have to start somewhere. Gradually people will see our point and warm up to our stoves.

Yours,

But he said:

Dear Cousin,

To compare us with Israel and Judah is your kind of mathematics, a fake balance achieved by paradox. One and one does not make two. One cannot add itself to one and make two, unless it never was One before. Because a One is One and Two is also One. So we can say logically one and one and one and one ad infinitum, but all other mathematics is for business, and our business is not to count. The pleasure of a shorter nose, or of having a chin and cheek where there have been none, cannot be measured, and occasionally you too must enjoy writing words for the fun of it and not just for money. I have given it some considerable thought, dear Cousin, and suggest we should get out of stoves right away. There is nothing we can do right now but wait and pray and be charitable to others. Giving people your kind of warmth, the so-called "real warmth," will cost them money, and even if it does *them* any good, it doesn't mean people will do good to others. A man's good deeds cannot be counted; only in his love for his fellowman does he find his reward. By loving even your enemy, you will have no enemy, for all love is God's. But if you do not believe this, love itself will become your enemy and tear your soul apart with jealousy and lust. All your doings should be unconcerned with your own well-being and all your life should be a service to your fellow man. This is how to return love to God as if it were the most excellent dish of Oriental cuisine, a feeling that will warm your heart better than a sauna or a Dutch stove. Of course I am not against the business you propose in principle, only in practice.

Yours,

I was angry with him and wrote:

Dear Buci,

I like your beautiful ideas and the fine words you wrap them in, but what good are they to us? The question is not: If, but when. If we can wait forever, as you seem to think, why go into business, yet you yourself are not against it in principle, though *you think* you are, even if you don't say so, in so many words. You are against it in principle, this has now become clear. Essentially you are an anti-revolutionary, conservative, semi-mystical Pole, whereas I am a practical, realistic, pragmatic, progressive Pole. And in spite of our Jewish background we are Catholics, something only insiders can understand. Living with Catholics made us catholic, and our Jewish references are the traditional jargon. If we look closer I can even detect in you an Orthodox Russian and in myself the Roman. Had we been communists, I would be Trotsky and you Stalin, if atheists, you would have called me a fascist or a Lutheran, and I would have called you a Jesuit. But this is not the point I want to debate: The principle is the principle—you might be correct in the long run, but I insist that we have to look at the situation as it now exists, not as it will be ultimately, not as it is beyond the ordinary confines of time and space. Our ordinary perceptions show clearly that all mystical expectations are wondrous fairytales of things to come, whereas searching our souls for what we can do now for our fellow man leads me to believe that love is not an abstract notion, not a smile and a kind word. It might be this too, but above all it is some of the fire that warms the body, the container of man's soul for the price of a fig.

Yours,

He immediately wrote me:

Dear Cousin,

Anything that is not a timeless proposition is a waste of time. If our stoves make us rich, you will think we deserve it. Yet a good man cannot be rich. It becomes the evildoer to be rich, not the good man. It is not the evil man who suffers pain in extracting his neighbor's debts, it is the good man who suffers. But if you suffer the pain of the other instead of sharing your joy with him, you are not rich, but a pauper. If suffering is in the soul, so is wealth. You might say, "Nonsense, just don't suffer in your soul. Look after your body. When all men live reasonably well, all is well. Is the need for the basics of a good life less important than the need for God?" I will remain outside the gates and this discussion. I cannot enter the gates of a town called peace that was conquered with blood and not with reason.

Maybe in a few years all the world will come to you and order the best stoves in the world, providing the people can trust your message. But who will trust in the wisdom of a running man who hurries down into his abyss as if chased by evil spirits? You are my cousin, and if you make a fool of yourself, people blame me. The other day, just to test your idea, I stopped a man in the street and told him there is something better in the world than his stove. He said, "Why not?" and went on his way.

                                             Yours,

P.S. A propos mathematics: Try to extract the base root of zero and add it to the greatest common denominator and see what you get. After you have done that, try to multiply yourself a billion times and subtract the sum from the sum total of all numbers. You'll be surprised by what you find.

   I then fired this back to him:

Dear Buci,

   I like your letters, but I don't agree with you. You see all things in terms of eternity. If we compared all our actions with the timeless time of the Lord, we would never do anything ourselves, but would merely wait for what comes to us. I believe in free will, I believe we can decide, plan, act exactly as we wish. You don't really understand what Christians, Jews and Muslims mean by God Almighty. You come nearest to the ancient Muslims by believing as they do that nothing can happen without Allah's will, but even Muslims think now in new Christian-Marxist-Jewish-Modern terms. You seem more pious than our forefather Abraham, who embodies the archaic past, the dawn of civilization, the beginning of enlightenment, but lived before the

new conscience of Isaac, awoke, before the even newer spirit
called Jacob who struggled with God, won, and who was blessed
as "Israel," which means fighter with God. So, after all, our
grandfather is inside your skin. His belt must have hit you hard,
while I, alas, never met our grandfather and thus escaped
his belt.

Your apparent strength is your true weakness, while my
weakness might well be the fanaticism with which I pursue my
idea. First of all, we are not dealing here with religious but with
practical problems. I need money to live, you need money to live.
There are stoves. There are customers. All we need is to get
them together. Let's not speak in parables, let's discuss quantities
and qualities. Let's talk terms. What are your conditions to throw
up plastic surgery and join me in my new enterprise? You are
my cousin and mustn't let me down. It soon will be spring.

Yours,

I waited and waited and finally it came:

Dear Cousin,

I have stated my terms; I have told you what I think. No
stoves. No business. I will go on repairing faces with plastic
and you stick to your accounting. You call it writing; have it your
way. I am neither our grandfather nor our forefather Abraham.
It's all in your head. Like you I believe in free will, which, free
as a wild horse, follows the instinct that leads it to ever greener
pastures. But a free will that is conscious is no longer free; it is
a will bound by supposition, by presumption, ideals, and wishful
thinking. Nothing good ever came of it. Idealists are not always
good people, and it is ethics—nothing else—that keeps the
world of man together. And ethics tells us that we must not
struggle but be led.

Indeed Israel received the blessing, and it still needs a shield
made of iron to defend it. This shield of iron is not as strong
or as impenetrable as the shield I suggest you arm yourself with.
In the name of all saints, Jewish, Catholic, Muslim and Hindu,

in the name of all saints, black, white, or yellow—in the name
of all martyrs and heroes of the Resistance, of all those who
died, as if their life would be nothing more than a smile returned
to a friend, I suggest you take your idea and make a story out of
it, for I will not enter this business. You would have to do it all
on your own. Yet, just to show I am your brother once removed,
I stopped a woman who was looking at stoves in a shop window
and asked her whether she wants a new, a better, a cheaper
stove. She said she was tired and I shouldn't pester her.

Yours,

      I ran to the postbox with this:

Dear Buci,
    My impression is you have no idea how to talk to pros-
pective customers. Don't talk to people in the street. I regret I
ever suggested this. You must enter their homes, remove what
they have, and leave them your number. If a customer protests,
pay him what he asks. Thus you can buy his opinion and leave
him with new hope. Why not do the same with a stove? He has
to be convinced to buy even when he doesn't need it immediately, for thus he will help the workers who live by the manufacture of the unnecessary. We will still only make a profit small
enough not to burden our consciences too heavily. Don't offer
anything you are not prepared to see installed in his home, try
to get him to make up his mind beforehand by offering more
money for his old wreck than he ever dreamed of seeing in his
lifetime. Incidentally, we could sell the secondhand stoves to pay
the first invoice on the new one. I too have had my first customer. A two-faced lady who lives neither above nor below. She
came from somewhere else and had no address. Still I found her
and when I delivered the stove, she broke out in laughter. We lit
it for her but she still went on laughing, and as soon as we had
warmed up her place, she left and disappeared into the cold
night. Fortunately, I took her money first so she will return
when she feels more serious. I enclose the money so you can

give it to one of your charities. Donate it to the community, throw it into the sea, give it to the government, which is poorer than both of us.

Yours,

And this is what he sent back:

Dear Cousin,

I handed your cheque over to the local soup kitchen, a wise investment. You never know, we both might need a friend there one day. I met another man in the street, a type who looks for new energy resources, and he agreed that looking over the stove would not harm him. But all I could show him was a picture of the stove. Besides, he said he had to consult his family before making any new purchases. I asked him to return for the instructions and diagram. The stove he will get in the next world, I presume.

Everyone is on strike. People no longer wish to work, for any amount of money in the world. If my man does not come back by next week, you can save yourself the cost of shipment.

Yours,

P.S. He came back before I could mail this letter and said all right, let's have one of those. For a deposit he left me his hand-carved gold teeth. I will put them in a safe and give my share to my favorite charity, a fund for retired circus horses, and hand yours to the government, which will please you, no doubt. Congratulations. In spite of myself, in spite of all my objections, I found a customer and you found at least one. Before we knew it, we were right in the middle of it all, and now things look more promising than ever. I have changed my mind because of this first success, and now I'm ready to go into business with you after all. I will throw away my plastic and tell my patients to take their noses and wrinkles somewhere else. I am ready to quit everything. I am convinced it doesn't matter whether we save the human soul, the main thing is to save ourselves and have a good time. Now that I have turned around, I am certain you, too, will have changed your mind. Let me know when the sample arrives.

Yours,

So I finally told him:

Dear Buci,

The sample is ready to be shipped, and only needs dismantling before packaging. The boxes I ordered turned out to be too small, and to order larger ones would take too long, so I decided to take them apart and make a smaller parcel. To dismantle them is a longer job than you might think. I had a few men working on it night and day, but everyday they wanted more money until finally I had to tell them to stop the work and leave. They've gone and now I have to find new people who won't begrudge me my profit. From you they must have learned that One added to another One cannot make Two.

Your customer, too, will have to wait. His gold teeth sound like a good surety, but wouldn't it have been wiser to take from him an arm or a leg so he won't run away? What if his teeth never fitted him anyway, and he wanted to get rid of them and they are neither gold nor brass, but painted cardboard? Would you know the difference? Anyway, I have to learn to wait as well. Customers are coming all day and night, but I can't help them. I rang up the factory to ask for delivery dates. It turned out I had made a small mistake. They only had this one stove that I gave to the laughing lady. Forget the stoves, forget the entire business. I will go back to my writing, but should I think of a new idea, I will get in touch with you, Special Delivery.

Yours,

The Cheat

ONCE UPON A TIME there was a King who divided his kingdom in two unequal parts. The larger share he gave to his firstborn son, the smaller to his second. The Queen loved the younger son more than her firstborn, because he never left her side, while her elder son was usually off hunting. Before the King died, he called both his sons to his deathbed to make known to them which part of the country would be left each. He said, "It is my will that the larger share, from the mountains to the sea, should belong to my elder son. To my second son I leave all the country that is neither mountain nor plain and is neither bordered by the sea nor by any river."

The younger son said, "So be it, my father," and the elder son said, "Your will is our command."

But the Queen was unhappy for her favorite son and cried, "You are cruel and unjust. One son is given all the country, and the other, whose land can be neither on the mountain nor in the plains nor bordered by either river or sea, is given the crevices in the soil and the sky above for his inheritance."

"This is my will," said the King. "You cannot change it."

"If I cannot change it," said the Queen, "I still will not accept it."

"Poor woman, what can you do?" asked the King, and he died and was buried.

A little later the younger brother called on the elder and said, "Our father left you all his land, but to me he left the holes in the furrows and the sky for my abode. How shall I live?"

"Become my tenant," said the older brother, and went off hunting.

The younger brother became his older brother's tenant and paid him an annual rent. Then one year famine struck the land, and the younger brother had nothing with which to pay his debts to his older brother.

"Never mind," said the elder, pay when you can." And once again he went off hunting.

A few years later an earthquake destroyed the younger brother's house, but as a tenant, he had to wait until his brother would build him a new one. Then came the rainy season and it was hard for the younger to endure the cold and dampness. He went to his brother and said, "When are you going to build me a new house? The rains are already here and soon it will snow."

"Stay in my house," said his older brother, "and be my guest."

Thus he moved into his brother's house, because the rains fell and he had no house of his own. He lived in the house of his brother as his guest. He came to the table when called and left when it was time to leave. He spoke when it was his turn and kept his tongue on a leash, because he was a guest of the house and did not wish to offend its owner.

When all went well in the country and there was plenty of venison and other game, peace and harmony ruled in the house. The guests ate with the owners and no one quarreled, but when there was a drought or a famine, a plague of locusts or some other misfortune, the older brother's wife would say, "Remember we have children of our own, we cannot let them starve. We must feed them first before we feed the family of your brother. Let him go and live in the sky or in the crevices—wherever his place may be—but let him leave here soon or we will all die of hunger."

"He is my younger brother," said her husband, "I will not let him die. We will all share equally among us." And so they did. It happened, however, that the youngest son of the older brother (who was now King) became gravely ill, because once again famine had entered the land and everyone was starving. It was then the Queen stepped in to save her youngest son. She said to her husband, "It is now time for you to tell your brother to leave, for his family will survive ours. He seems to be more hardened in survival, because the crevices in the earth and the sky are his home and he can withstand all the elements, while, as you can see, our youngest is dying."

"Then I will send him away."

"No," said his wife, "if you send him away, he might still eat from the fat of the earth and live, but this does not change the fate of our little one."

"What shall I do?" asked the King.

"You must kill him," she said.

"I would rather wait," said the King.

"If my little one dies my life is not worth living," said the Queen.

"If I kill my brother," said the King, "I will feel guilty. No, let him live and let him go where he belongs."

The younger brother and his family thus went back to the devastated land, though some of his family were slain, because the King's order not to kill his brother had gone out too late.

When the younger brother's family returned to the desert, of which most could remember nothing, many died of the hardships, but those who survived began to dig for water, found edible roots, and even an oasis with fresh water and palms with dates. Soon they began to use some of the water to irrigate the desert and make things grow and were thus able to live quite comfortably.

When the news reached the older brother that the younger

was neither starving nor hungry but living quite well, the King dispatched his messenger to order his brother to leave the oasis so the King's family might come down from the starving city to feed itself and live.

The younger brother sent back this message to his brother, the King: "You wanted me to leave your home; I did. You killed some of my family; I did not alter my course, but went to find a waterhole and a crumb of bread for the survivors. You can come and share with us what we have, but not all of you can come or we will be swamped by your family and drowned. You inherited the biggest share of our father's domain, but you have not inherited the entire earth. Send some of your dying down to us and we will nourish them back to life. Send some of your weak and poor and we'll help them—we'll teach them to find food and water in the desert. But if you send all of them, there will be a struggle for life and death between us, and as we are smaller in number than you, it is we who will die, who will lose our lives, and this was not the will of our father. He allotted me a share in this world, if only a small one because I was born after you, but as I am his son, he wanted me to live, and my mother loved me more than you, as your wife, the Queen, loves her youngest more than her eldest."

Back came the reply: "We are coming all the same." And the King came with his family to occupy the oasis, the only source of life left in the country. When his men arrived they found the place empty. There was not a soul about. The family of the younger brother had buried itself in crevices or taken to the sky. The elder brother took over everything and believed he now ruled all the world. There was no one to blame if he suffered a misfortune, and no one who might envy him his share. So the world was ruled by the older brother and under his kingship it was united and strong, or so he thought. After a while, however, as time went by and his crops failed, he blamed himself and cursed the world and everything around him became dark. He could find no pleasure in life and even cursed God for having created him. When he heard his brother's voice in the pitch black of his darkness, he said, "How can you still speak to me, when I cannot see you?"

"Listen," said the voice of his brother, "It is too late now. I told you not to send your family down, so you might still have a place of refuge for your sick and dying, but now the earth is your refuge and if you fail, you have no one to blame but yourself."

"So you did not die," said the King. "You are either buried or in heaven, but I can hear your voice."

"Yes," said the younger brother, "I can still speak and you can still hear me, that's why they call me Jacob or the cheat."

The Lie

ONCE UPON A TIME there was a King who asked two people to his court—a man and a woman.

"Would you like to work for me?" asked the King. The man said yes, and his wife said she would help her husband. So they worked for the King and lived well and prosperously.

One day, the woman was reading a book in which was written, "The King of a country asked two people to come to his court and work for him, and so they did and they lived prosperously and happily, but he did not tell them that this would only be for a short while and not forever." The woman told her husband that she had learned that the King had not told them that they would work for him only for a short while.

The husband said, "What do you want me to do?"

"Nothing," said the woman, "I only wanted to tell you what I have read."

"Why did you have to tell me what is only known to you?" said the man. "Now I will always be unhappy and unable to enjoy my prosperity."

"That's true," said the woman, "but at least you know."

The husband was never again happy and never able to enjoy his prosperity, because his wife had told him what she had read and he blamed her for her knowledge of what he should not have known. Later, he confiscated all her books and would not let her read another, afraid she might tell him that he might not even be alive and therefore had nothing to worry about.

"Why do you take my books?" asked the woman. "They are just words."

"It's with words," said the man, "that you lied to me when you told me it is written somewhere that this life is not forever, and the King had deceived us by not telling us the truth when he asked us to work for him at his court. But the King does not lie when he does not reveal the truth. You must not believe what you read."

"I don't wish to live with lies," said the woman, "and I want us both to know the truth so we are ready to leave when the time comes."

"I was never anything but ready," said the man, "and can only do what the King tells me."

But he, too, lied and the woman knew it, although she never mentioned her knowledge to him again and thus gave him a short time of peace. The woman herself wrote to the author of the book, "Why did you write that the King is not telling the truth; how do you know the truth?" But she never received an answer and still waits for it.

The Theft

A MAN tied his horse to a tree and thought, I will sit next to my horse and keep my eyes open, so no one will steal it. I must not sleep even if I'm tired. He stayed awake for two days, four days, then on the sixth day he fell asleep and a thief came and stole his horse. When our man woke up and saw that the horse was gone, he at first blamed himself for not staying awake, but finally admitted that no man could keep awake forever to guard his property. So he went in search of what had been stolen from him. After three days walk he met a man riding his horse. The horse recognized its owner and threw the rider and once again the owner was mounted on his horse while the thief went on foot. After a while the man on horseback took pity on the thief and offered to let him sit behind him on the horse's back. They rode like this for a while, until a steep hill had to be climbed and the horse refused to carry them both up the slope. The two men took turns walking next to the horse until the slope descended, when again both of them sat in the saddle.

In the distance, on the horizon, they saw herds of wild stallions. "Why don't you catch one of these wild horses," the man asked the thief.

"I cannot," said the thief. "I never learned how to do that."

"But you can't ride with me forever," said the man. "I am tired of your company."

"Just take me to town," said the thief. "I know a bank that I can rob, and with the money I will hire a man who will catch me a horse."

"Can't you earn money?" asked the man. "Do you have to rob a bank?"

"Yes," said the thief. "I never learned to make money; that's why I have to take it from those who know how to earn it."

In town, the thief thanked the man for the ride and dismounted. He entered a bank, killed the owner, took the money and disappeared. He was just leaving the town, the money hidden in his clothes, when he again met the man whose horse he had stolen.

"Now that I have money," he said, "will you sell me your horse? You can catch another one."

"How did you get the money?" asked the man.

The thief told him that he had killed the banker and taken all the money he could lay hands on.

"I must not help you any more," said the man. "I am guilty of having brought you here to kill a man and steal his money."

"But you did a good deed by not letting me walk," said the thief, "or I might have died of exhaustion and you would have me on your conscience. Now it's me who's killed a man, not you."

"Here, take my horse," said the man, "and don't pay me for it."

The man dismounted from his horse and watched the thief ride off. He went to sleep under a tree, happy to have regained his peace of mind.

The Near Murder

ONCE UPON A TIME there lived a very old man, who had a wife who was also very old, but no children. They had everything they needed—houses, gardens, food, wine, money—they owned horses, cattle and dogs, plantations, fishing grounds and deep woods. They were healthy, strong, wise and beloved by everyone in the country. They had everything but children, and they were sad.

The woman said to the man: "I met a stranger yesterday who told me I will have a child before I die."

"What did you say?" asked the husband.

"I laughed," said the woman.

"Why did you laugh?" asked her husband.

"Because I am old," she said, "and an old woman cannot have a child. That's why I laughed."

"Pity that you laughed," said the man.

"Why?"

"Because the stranger might have been someone who knows more than you and I do," said the man.

And so it was. The woman became pregnant and bore her husband a son. Their happiness was now complete. One day, the man was returning from his work and as he walked home, he heard a voice behind him. "Take your son," said the voice, "and kill him." When the man turned around, there was no one there who could have spoken to him.

How can I kill my son, he asked himself. What an insane idea. But again the voice spoke in his ear and said, "Kill your son," and this before he entered his house.

"Why are you sad now?" asked his wife.

And he told her what the voice had said to him.

The woman wept. What else could she do? Her husband was lord over everyone in the area and he would not listen to her anyway.

One morning he asked his son to go out with him. "Take your gun," he said, "we are going hunting."

"What kind of game?" asked the son.

But the old man said nothing, just walked silently, his eyes cast down, his gun slung across his shoulder. When they reached the wood, the man said to his son, "I have to listen to an inner voice and this voice has told me to kill you."

The son could see no way out of the forest, which also belonged to his father, and as men with guns at the ready were all over the place, he knew that this was his end. "All right," he said to his father, "go ahead and shoot me."

The father tied his son to a tree, lifted his gun and was about to pull the trigger when a voice behind him said, "Don't be insane. I just wanted to know whether you were ready to kill him, as I see you are. Let him go and kill a goat instead." The old man suddenly saw a goat not far away, which hadn't been there before. The goat had caught its horns in a thicket and was struggling to get away. The father aimed his gun at the goat and killed it. Then, without a word, he untied his son, and together they walked back silently to their home. The woman was happy to see her son alive, for she had given up hope.

Later that night, she asked her husband: "Why did you behave so insanely? Why did you want to kill him?"

"It was not him I wanted to kill, it was your doubt. It was your laughter I wanted to destroy."

"And you didn't," said the woman.

"No I didn't," said the man, "a voice told me I should let him live."

The name of the son was Isaac—which means laughter—and he later inherited all of his father's estates and lived to a ripe old age.

The King and
His Five Sons

ONCE UPON A TIME there was a King who had five sons, but one of them, the eldest, was blind. The King was in constant mourning because of the misfortune that had befallen him and his eldest son. He consulted many doctors from all corners of the earth, but the doctors could do nothing for his son. "He has no eyes," said one, without trying to open his lids; "he has no optical nerve," said another, without trying to stimulate it; "he has no vision because he looks inward," said a third, without trying to make him reverse his gaze. "He has no idea what the world looks like," said the fourth, without telling him what it did look like. The fifth just stated categorically that the son pupils so the light in his eyes was diffused and he could not see a thing, and gave him no help to concentrate the light through a finer point.

When the King had listened long enough to the doctors, he sent them all packing and asked for the magicians to be brought. They came from all four corners of the earth, loaded with tools and charms, all kinds of sticks and wands and other geometric paraphernalia. "Aye," said the first magician, the magician of the North, "I can see his trouble right away. Put an icecap on his forehead; when it melts, his sight will be restored.

"Go ahead," said the King, "get an icecap. I'll pay for it."
"I need the biggest icecap in the world," said the Magician
of the North.

"Will the North Pole do?" asked the King, and he ordered
him the North Pole.

The Magician put the North Pole and all its ice on the
blind man's head and waited for it to melt. After a long or
perhaps it was a short time, the North Pole melted, but the
son's eyes did not open. He was still as blind as before.

"Kill the liar," said the King. And they killed the Magician
of the North.

"What's your trick?" asked the King, when they brought
the Magician of the West to his court.

"I'll make your son repeat my magic formula and spit
three times into each direction of the wind. That is twelve
times all together, and he will then be able to see."

"Go ahead," said the King, "make him repeat your magical
formula and make him spit as you like, but not in my eye."

"Why not?" asked the Magician of the West. "Just this one
spitting might cure him, he might want to spit into his father's
eye more than in any other direction."

"All right," said the King, "let him spit in my eye as
well, just make him see, that's all I ask of you."

So the Magician from the West walked with the blind man
out into the fields and made him repeat the names of all the
holy books of the West three times, as a magic formula. After
a certain time had passed, this too was accomplished, and all
that was left was the spitting. The blind man spit three times
to the North—nothing happened; three times to the South—
and nothing happened; three times he spit right into the face
of the Magician, who stood in the West, and even that didn't
help him; finally he spit three times to the East. It was like
the sound of three raindrops in a monsoon.

Nothing. Not even a slight improvement. "Ah, but you can
also spit in your father's face." The blind man at first refused,
but as the King encouraged his son, in order that he might

gain his eyesight, the son finally managed to do this outrageous thing. But nothing happened.

"You are a charlatan," said the King, "and not a magician. Your words are nonsense and your ideas sterile. I don't even want to kill you. Go ahead and live, but out of my sight."

The Magician of the South had been waiting for this, and jumped forward. "Can you see this stick?" he asked the King.

"I can," said the King, "but he can't. Cure him. Make him see. You are the Magician of the South, maybe you are cleverer than your friends."

"Would you mind if I take this stick and hit him on the head with it until his eyes pop out? They will open up after the beating I give him. Please give me permission to do this."

"Ask my son," said the King.

"You can beat me as much as you like," said the blind son, "just don't kill me. I don't mind if it hurts a bit at first, as long as I can see afterwards."

"Well observed," said the Magician of the South, whose tongue was as suave as his stick was rough. He hit the blind man once. The blind man's head shook, his brains tumbled, he nearly swallowed his tongue and forgot to breathe, but nothing happened.

"Let me do this properly now," said the magician. He made a heavy swipe as with a sword and literally cut the blind man in a hundred places with so many strokes, but even these wounds healed in good time and still nothing happened.

"Let's try it once more," said the Magician of the South. He threw the blind man to the floor, first beat his flesh to a pulp, then broke each of his bones with his own hands (he was strong and could easily do it). And although the blind man lay there apparently dead, he recovered even from this nightmare of the South, but still without being able to see a hand in front of his eyes.

The King, who had put much hope in the Magician of the South, but without ever mentioning it to anyone, was more than disappointed. He was furious. He had the Magician of

the South put into an oven in which the flames shot up sky
high, and there he left him long enough to become charred
black. The King then made him come out, but put him back
again; still he wouldn't let him be consumed by the flames,
as he felt that death was too kind a reward for this swindler
who had done nothing but break the poor blind man's bones
without giving him anything in return.

"There is only one left, the Magician of the East," said
the King. "And by now I am disappointed for nothing can
possibly work. My son is blind, and he will stay blind, the
poor bastard." (The King's language was sometimes rather
rough, probably to hide his tender love for the son of his
misfortune).

The Magician of the East had waited his turn patiently and
now he smiled at the King and said, "Leave him to me for an
hour, Sir. I will open his third eye, if I can't open the other
two, so at least he will see something and probably more than
we can with two."

"Brilliant," said the King, "open his third eye. Just make
him see."

The Magician of the East went into a trance and called
up all the ancestors of the blind man, back to his being merely
the thought of an idea of a thought which was less or more
than nothing of something that is nothing but peace, beauty,
harmony and tranquility. He did this three times, going back
and forth with him through all the generations of men and
animal, plant and stone, atoms and nucleii of atoms. "Can you
see what I can see?" asked the Magician of the East. He had to
repeat the question. Everyone in the court held his breath.

"Yes," said the blind man, "I can see."

"What do you see," asked the King, when he heard the
good news, "what do you see, my son?"

"I see everything with my third eye," said the son.

The Magician of the East smiled and refused a fee or
reward.

"I can see the peace and tranquility, the beauty and harmony of all the universes," shouted the son, and no one seemed to notice that his eyes were as locked as before. After all, he was supposed to see all this with the third eye, as only the magicians in the East can do.

The King was about to arrange for the biggest banquet of his entire life and had sent out all the invitations, when he received the bad news that his son, who so recently had regained his sight, had lost his life because he had crossed the street against a red traffic light and had been hit by a Ford Mustang. He could not possibly have seen it with his third eye.

"That's the Magician of the East," said the King, "he takes neither fee nor reward for his magic. His only reward is seeing a blind man dead." And the King went into a long period of mourning.

When this was over, he said to himself, "I must remember my other sons: The one who is deaf, the one who cannot speak, the one who can neither taste nor smell and the one who has no feelings." But he never again asked doctors, magicians, philosophers or stargazers to his court, and he left his sons as they were born, incurable and incomplete.

The Story of
Lilith and Eve

*B*EFORE *God created Eve, the legend tells us, he created Lilith, but Lilith left Adam, as she could never agree with him in smaller and larger matters, and Eve became Adam's true wife, that is, a woman who is always in agreement with her man. Lilith left, but Lilith didn't leave for good, for she returns to haunt Adam as lust, the legend tells us.*

نح

O*NCE UPON A TIME* there was a man who was haunted by Lilith. The demon has disguised herself in the clothes of an ordinary, simple, agreeable woman and came to visit Adam when he was alone.

"Why are you on your own?" Lilith asked. "Where is your woman, the one who came to replace me?"

"She is out in the country where she went to visit relatives. She will return soon and she will not be pleased to find you here, for she fears you."

"Why should my sister be afraid of me?" asked Lilith. "I am as simple in my heart as she is, I am as good and kind as she is, I love my parents and I love my children just as she does. But we don't think alike—our difference between us is in our minds, not in our bodies."

"I believe you," said Adam, "and I love you, but I need a peaceful life."

"Have it your way," said Lilith, "have your peaceful life. I am just your other woman. I will not leave you but love you as I always did."

Adam looked into her eyes and said no more. Her eyes were like doors wide open into a world he had nearly forgotten, and he stepped inside.

They were in each other's arms and mouths when Eve returned. "Lilith and Adam are united," she said. "Stay with me, sister. I will bring food to your bed." She brought to their bed food and drink both, and retired to a far corner of the house, where she crouched beside the stove to keep herself warm and went into a trance. She left her body and entered the body of her sister Lilith, and thus she embraced and kissed Adam and felt his love for her as she had never known it before.

"But I am your Eve," said Lilith, "why do you love me so passionately, as you have never loved me with such passion before?"

Adam laughed and said, "You will leave with dawn and I will not see you for a while. If I am passionate, it's because our happiness is for but a short time."

"How can you say that?" said Lilith. "I will be here tomorrow and the day after and so for the rest of your life. Why do you love me so passionately? Do you think I am who I appear to be? I am Eve, speaking through my sister's mouth."

"You are joking," laughed Adam. "I know you will leave at dawn and will not be back for a long time."

Lilith (who was now Eve) kissed him and said, "I wish this were so, but alas I cannot leave you. I will stay with you because you are full of fire for this other woman whose body I have taken over. Look at me carefully and tell me whether you don't see that I am your wife, Eve?"

"Eve sits in the far corner of the house," said Adam, but when he looked, he could not see his wife. What he saw were merely the flames from the stove.

The Beauty of a
Plastic Showcase

*N*OAH *had three sons — Ham, Shem and Japhet*

ᘓ⁊

Oɴᴄᴇ ᴜᴘᴏɴ ᴀ ᴛɪᴍᴇ there lived a man who had extraordinary sight. He saw everything. Nothing, he believed, ever escaped any of his five senses, but especially not his sight. While others could hardly distinguish an elephant from a mosquito, this man saw, not the mosquito as tiny and the elephant as large, but each in its true proportion to the other. He had certainly seen light in a rare perspective, but when he tried to tell his friends what he saw, he was either greeted with sneers, mockery, and laughter, or worse, with yes and amen and anything you say, sir, because he was too clear for them. What good is my sight to me, he wondered, if whatever I see is either accepted or disbelieved, it makes little difference which. What's the point of it all? I had better ask the Owl.

"It's difficult," said the Owl. "You are in a bad way, my dear. If others do or do not believe what you see, and it makes no difference to you, you might better be blind than a seer."

"Thank you," said the man to the Owl, "I wish you had wiser things to say. If people acted in accordance with what I see, they would arrest most world politicians, hijack or kidnap them, each country taking care of its own kings, ministers, priests, kings' advisers, generals and retainers of the court. Not that they would be killed, far from it, but treated as patients, very kindly and gently, as if one were their nurse, mother and best friend, so to speak, and gradually they would be nursed back to sanity. But who will act out this fantasy, I ask you?"

"You never know," said the Owl. "You never know what will happen sooner or later."

"To act," said the man, "they would have to act now while I am still alive and well and not when I am dead and buried. Where now are the men and women who would arrest their ministers and kings, their court retainers and generals, with kindness of spirit, lovingly, and with good feeling at heart?"

"Wouldn't such men and women rightly be called mad?" asked the Owl.

"Rightly called mad by whom? Don't make me laugh. Do you, the wisest of animals, hold man to be madder than we know him? I came for advice, not for diagnosis, Owl."

"You don't need advice," said the Owl, "all you need is to bide your time and sooner or later, as I said before—it doesn't matter."

"Thank you," said the man and went home.

$$\mathfrak{D}\!\!\!\!\backslash\!\!\backslash$$

He went home still burdened with his problem of clear sight. His wife could help him only with her love, but even this love (though gladly accepted by both as a great present from Him who has such presents to share) was not the end and the beginning of the universe, he thought, though it might well seem to be so for those who see none of the other colors of the spectrum, but only those that are usual. This man, who was so enlightened that he could see more than all the other receivers of light, realized he still had a problem. He might have to be ready to give his life in exchange for the fulfillment of his dream. Although he believed that acting on insight would be a forgone conclusion, he considered the Owl's suggestion that ultimately nothing matters, nothing is worth serious consideration.

He decided to take the matter to the Fox, whom he had liked for calling grapes not within his reach sour. He also liked the Fox for stirring up hunters—fancily dressed fools, who believe they can bag anything but their folly (until the day they drop all guns into the rivers)—and he liked the Fox for his courage in outwitting the hunters, knowing only too well that they are bereft of mercy.

"So that's where you live," said the man, when he finally found the Fox in his burrow. "It looks to me as if you are living in the twenty-second century."

"What do you mean?" asked the Fox. "Do you think in 150 years everyone will have a hole in the ground with a lid to cover him in case he ceases to breathe? You are an optimist! The way I see it is, there will be more, many more than one to a hole. I thank the Maker for the hunters' aim or we might have had to emigrate to Canada."

"O Fox," the man said, "whom are you trying to fool? Do you really think it's better to be dead than to be alive with too many relatives? Is not all mankind related in some way?"

"That's no question," said the Fox. "Why don't you ask me your question instead. I have much time for thinking between runs, not only while I wait for the hunter, but also while hunting myself to help the chickens with their problem. This too needs some thought and planning."

"One question, Fox: The Owl says it ultimately doesn't matter, as sooner or later all things that have to take their place in time will surely find it. Shall I believe the Owl?"

"I certainly would," said the Fox, "if I were as wise as she is, but wisdom is not what I need as urgently right now as to

brace myself for my daily labor. My working day consists of
running and resting and thinking in between. I cannot give you
wisdom; instead, I can give you some practical advice on how to
avoid its pitfalls. With wisdom you may live four thousand
million years, which is neither wise nor advisable. The way I
see your situation is a matter of geometry—a question of
exact location and a matter of good navigational instruments.
Before you find yourself with more time than you might want
or need, you must first find yourself the space you want to
play in. Hunting is the way of life that is good for your adrenalin,
good for digestion, good for your offspring. You get more of
everything, so to speak, if you are on the run. Imagine yourself
being chased up and down hill forever and, I dare say, the lord
of this estate finds it particularly displeasing, as he notices
how all his foxes thrive on getting killed and killing smaller
prey. Consider," said the Fox, "that you have, in fact, only
one problem, which is how to get used to the condition and
smile."

"It's all right for foxes," said the man, "and if I were one
of your kind, I would certainly listen to you. Thanks all the
same."

"Thank you," said the Fox, "I like to see a man who has
no problem."

∽

In his own heart, the man knew neither the Owl nor the
Fox had the answer to his problem, which is nonexistent if
you don't see it. He laughed to himself and thought, if I go to
any of my four friends—the tasters, touchers, listeners, smellers
—who know everything just as well as I do, I will have no
answer and no problem either, but then I might as well be
someone else. Whereas if I take advice of the animals, whom I
admire for their natural ability to accept the inevitable from
their hunters and masters with such apparent grace, I would
have to become one of them. He contemplated a visit to the

powerful eagle, the strong lion, the eternal tortoise, the silent
fish, the kind doe, and the peaceful pigeon, to find power and
strength, eternity and silence, kindness and peace, but felt he
wouldn't be satisfied anyway. "I will cease to see so much," he
said to his wife, but his wife said that this too would be folly.
He decided to go to the desert and talk to the wind.

ℑ⟩

The wind didn't say much the first two or three years, and
after the seventh or eighth it began to dawn on him that the
city he had fled so he could be alone in his mind, this city
saw the same sun rise and set, but with a million more eyes.
The light that had been upon him in abundance when he
measured it amid the light of others seemed suddenly to retreat
into a darkness, as if he could not longer behold more than
his share. His need, he decided, was to search out the solution
as the Fox had suggested and the Owl had confirmed.

ℑ⟩

After seven or eight years in the untouched womb, in
virginal sands, neither opened up nor closed off to a suitor, he
dreamed of flowers and other pleasures the city provides, as
before in town he had dreamed of salvation in solitude. He
began to make his way back to the city, and when he arrived
within its walls, he could hardly recognize it. All and everything had changed. Every house had its garden and every garden
its fruit trees; everyone had enough of everything and no one
wished for more. Rulers, priests, retainers of the court, the
generals and even the magicians were kept in beautiful nursing
homes, watched day and night by intelligent and efficient doctors
of medicine and philosophy, and pampered with love and kisses
by the most beautiful women in town. There was no killing
and there were no foxes, no wisdom and no owls, no silence
and no fish. There was noise and hustle, but there was no

peace and no kindness, nor was there any eternity to speculate on. Doe, pigeon and tortoise had disappeared, and what it looked like to him now was something he had seen but not believed, believed but not held possible, held possible but not thought necessary to excite himself about.

ﬦ

In the city his fellow men had not changed essentially, but something else had: his own sense of proportion. After seven or eight years in the desert, he now believed himself to know nothing and to have seen no more and possibly less than others. His enlightened friends were not surprised to find him talking to God one evening.

ﬦ

"God," said the man, "I know I know nothing and I don't wish to know more than I know, except one thing: When you abolished the killing between men in the few years I didn't watch what was going on here, you did it behind my back. When I saw your dawn come up alone without other eyes watching it with me, I believed you were treating me to a private experience, thus I prayed for private blessings. Now I again can see what kind of city it has become—one that knows no kindness, no silence and no peace, neither killing nor wanton evil. I pray you not to change this town when I am not here to see it."

God did not at first want to talk to the man until the man had shown he was serious in talking to Him. So He asked him for a little lamb—a bargain, one could say, yet a small, loveable, beautiful little animal, not yet grown to its full strength. What choice did our man have? He sacrificed his innocent little lamb of naivety to find out something he hadn't known before.

"Look," said God, "you know who I am and I know you. I am something you understand and something you love. I give you what you need and what you need is not to know what you don't know and not to see what you don't see. While people war, they make peace, and when they kill, they die. They don't die from natural death, but from killing. So I allowed men to kill each other until they were afraid they would die out. Then they stopped the killing of their own accord. With everyone who kills, I play games; with everyone who dies in peace, I am a holy and solemn God. I figured, let them laugh less and learn to have better control over their facial muscles. Why make grimaces? It's not the natural, normal expression of a face at rest. After the last war I stopped laughing. And men stopped with me. Now they are more practical. They have sobered up. Isn't that improvement enough?"

"What shall I do instead of laugh and cry? Be angry and roll my eyes, Lord?"

"Look at the situation," said God to this man, "if you distort your face in either way, you can cause storm and havoc, you can make tornadoes with your eyebrows. A single cough might fling a continent into the sea; anger makes for volcanoes. It's *you* who does this, man, not me. The reason I can't perform any miracles while you watch is because of a bad human habit I am about to correct. You read wrongly all the sayings. The teaching of reading and writing will become again a privilege of the elite alone, but this time the elite will not be envied for its knowledge. Its power will be curtailed by my will to make them even better men."

"How good do you want us, Lord?"

"Good enough to bring back the kindness of the doe and the silence of fish, good enough to bring back what was lost in the rush to leave the animals' world. I especially created against wanton killing, in new synthetic wrapping, in plastic containers, this wonderful clever machinery, these helpful hands of steel, useful ovens to fire you to courage, this gilded and chromed supermarket-junket-billboard-ping-pong-slot machine-television world. If you look carefully you will see it works, but be open to realities, not to a vision of times to come. What I want to happen now takes place now. The future will depend on realizing all the special blessings I gave their junk culture now. You notice how happy people are with an iron or a small transistor? Or a little Cadillac? Or a camera? Compare it to the olden days, when people needed slaves and palaces to feel well. They appear happier with less, it seems. Skyscrapers are no Babylon. Babylon could survive neither earthquake nor fire. It disintegrated because no one knew how to live in it properly. Now, in seven or eight years, men have learned to live together, but their nature is admittedly still violent and somewhat stupid. But soon I will inspire them to invent a new gadget to be clamped on one's earlobe when one is born. It's a small earring made of gold or any other metal which will pierce the ear with a fairly faint sound, a kind of melody that reaches all the membranes of the body. This will do the trick. He who does not wear this little ring with which I put him in chains, but removes it voluntarily, will be called insane and an outcast and be locked up, just like your insane man is now locked away."

"When is this going to happen, Lord?"

"It's happening right now, if you look carefully."

♫

"How can I make small earrings that filter a certain chemical through, in a very slow flow that one might speed up by twisting the pin that pierces the lobe like an acupuncture needle? Who is going to manufacture this thing?" the man asked himself. "I'd like to have one myself."

♫

A short time later our man (Japhet) met Shem and said to his brother, "Do you know anything about making small golden earrings filled with a certain chemical that allows God's counsel to be infused along with music?"

"Never heard of it," said Shem.

"That's good. I will be the first one to explain it to you."

"Go ahead," said his brother.

"There are all kinds of aspects to this little rind and suggestion is not the least of them, as it hurts when your ear is being pricked. You won't forget the pain, even if later you think you have. When you go into the deeper vaults of your soul, you know what hurts where and why. Something replaces this pain. Sheer bliss. You believe you are being pierced with a kind inner voice at all times. How can it fail?"

"Very well," said his brother, "pierce my ear then. Let's see what it feels like to hear something else."

"I still have to invent it," said Japhet. "I could put an earring through your earlobe now and you'll believe in your good luck. What I want is to invent the earring that brings good luck, not just to you, but to all men by *looking at you*. In future, I would be able to see from afar whether you are a man of peace."

"What if I refused to wear it?" asked his brother.

"Refuse yourself knowledge! You would be considered insane and be put in a house of confinement because no one would understand you."

"Then let's invent this thing now," said Shem.

ॐ

They went off together for a while, and after much conversing, constructed the earring. Now all men wore rings in their earlobes, recognizing each other instantly as the perfect species of Creation. They would not harm one another and began to love their plastic neon television world with the eyes of farmers on their fields before harvest time.

ॐ

The perfection of everything got a bit too much for our man. The little gold ring with its superchemcial infusion of

divine grace and wisdom created boredom in his soul (he
rejoiced continuously in the Lord) and it became nearly unbear-
able. He went to see God again. This time he wouldn't go with
an innocent little lamb for sacrifice, but for additional informa-
tion, something more substantial than man's lie that his universe
had become a rather boring institution, which now-tamed
instincts had previously replenished with a flow of adrenalin.
How to revert back to this flow of consciousness? Instead of
becoming more knowledgeable as we age, he thought we must
show how young we really are, consider how *little* knowledge we
have.

ℐ

"My God," he said, "what madness. To know nothing is
futile. To know something, unsatisfying. And even *not* to know
nothing seems too much knowledge. What's your advice?"

"What's your sacrifice?" said God.

"What do you want? Everything I have? My house, my
children? My wife? My life? My bull for a whole offering? My
goat for my sins? What have I that you can use and I cannot? I
am ready to give up some of my indolence, Lord, which causes
me to become bored, which arouses my curiosity. Shall I
sacrifice curiosity?"

"It wouldn't help you much if you did, " said God. "If you
were not curious, you would be impertinent. It's better to try to
find out than claim you know. Let's think of something else.
How about converting moral energy into aesthetic energy? How
about showing the beauty that exists not only in the tranquility
of the face, but also in the more hidden depths of the eyes? It's
evidently not enough for you that people are good and decent
citizens, well meaning and helpful; not enough that they love
their neighbor as themselves; the time of justice is over. Now
you are ready to see the beauty of it all and not just on the
face of it but in the eyes. Make a new law that mandates an
hour of beauty a day for every citizen. The time has come to add

to the Sabbath. Provide an additional hour of rest a day. Or are you also bored on the Sabbath?"

"That's what I am talking about, Lord. I don't mind adding another hour a day to my Sabbath, but what shall I do with it?"

"You didn't understand the finer point, or if you did, you forgot it. When you meditate, you are busy. The Sabbath is meditation. The rest of the week is for the preparation of the house. If you now add an hour a day, you will see a beauty that is not boring, but you must alternate between work and rest or your work is rest and your hours of meditation hard work. Take *more* time for leisure if you are bored, not less."

"Anything else?" asked the man.

"Come back when you have meditated enough on your inquiries, man."

"Thank God, I always do," lied the man and went home.

ᴒᴎ

That is how man developed an additional sense beyond the five senses, beyond sight and hearing, taste, touch and smell—a sixth sense for which he had neither name nor image, neither form nor description. He knew it without knowing it, heard it without it making a sound, tasted it, yet it had no taste, touched it like air that cannot be touched, smelled it though it had no odor. This sense he called beauty. A new sense, for he had never discovered it before, or had only believed it to exist on the surface. A new sense that was not new, but acquired. The beauty of a plastic showcase was the new miracle.

ᴒᴎ

And Japhet must one day return to his brother Shem to dwell in his tents, to live together for good. Had Ham not seen his father Noah naked, he would not have to be his brother's slave forever. Ham, too, might not feel cursed forever with the affliction of seeing more than is good for him.